Rose
The Celtic Fairy

The Celtic Fairy, Vol. 1
by Warrior Danika

Introduction

On the sunniest of days, you can hear the laughter and singing of Rose and her sisters on the rugged cliffs perched high above the Celtic Sea. Merriment here was much like any other usual day as they tended to their mother's garden while dancing and singing. Four sisters surrounded by beauty and the love of this most unusual family.

The youngest, Rose, was unique in many ways, but particularly in the deep secret she and her sisters shared. One that came from family lineage, one that she and her sisters held ever so closely among them. A secret that would be revealed to only a few chosen, and only at the right time.

Love was the principal thing in all of their sparkling days and nights living in a modest white castle on these most lovely of Irish coastal cliffs. Especially for a young girl who's vision was of helping others that were waiting and her decision to answer to the beckoning of love and the calling on her life to bring light, joy and love to those who needed it the most.

Chapters

Rose
The Celtic Fairy

A white stone dwelling could be seen towering above the Celtic sea, situated upon magnificent Irish coastal cliffs. There, settled above the raging waters, three generations of Dinnegans had lived on this very spot, on this very land. They were a fruitful and plentiful family, uncommonly blessed throughout the years. There was always kinship and much love here. This is where a wee child named Rose made her first appearance. She was a tiny creature, her mother, Daylen, had chosen her name just the day before she was born, strolling in

the family's ivy framed garden. If this new little one
was of the fairy side of the family, she would be the
fourth daughter of Daylen that would be bestowed
this honour.

It is written in the legendary book of the Dinnegan
family, that once upon a time Rose's great, great
great grandfather Jory was hunting down by the
quarry where he met a woman in the forest. He
saw her as she was gathering herbs. She was
stunning with black hair and crystal blue eyes. Jory
fell instantly in love, and as she raised from her
berry gathering she saw him in the distance and
was smitten. Her name was Moriah, an elegant
creature, one who held a deep secret.

Moriah lived in a tiny cottage in the forest and Jory
would visit her bringing trinkets and angel cakes
from the local town bakery. When that first winter
was gone and the blossom of Spring was upon the
land, Jory asked her to marry him, for he had fallen
forever in love. Her response was a joyful yes! For
she had found her kindred one. Jory was elated.
And wouldn't the family be happy he had married
before twenty five stones of life, when after that it
strangely seems all hope of marriage is lost.

It took Jory time to prepare the white stone dwelling
that sat above the Celtic sea for her arrival and the

impending nuptial, but finally the time had come.

The wedding celebration commenced as the sun was setting behind the edge of the sea. Grandfather Jory and Moriah were forever joined in front of God and the whole town who were present to join in the celebration. On their first wedded night together, Jory waited patiently for a young nervous Moria. There was a secret that she had been keeping from him and she was not sure how to go about telling him.

Finally it was time, she proclaimed her love, turned her back to him and shyly dropped her gown to reveal, tucked under her ivory shoulder blades, velvety blue wings. She turned and caught his eyes as she slowly unfolded her glorious wings. They glistened as she stretched them forth, catching and reflecting the light from the candle lit room. Gasping, Jory realized that his newly betrothed was in fact, a fairy. He moved towards her and embraced her, reassuring her that she took his breath away and it was reason to be more in love with her, than ever before.

This was the beginning of an amazing journey. There was such intense love between them. It was agreed upon, that Moriah's secret was to be kept just as that, a secret, although promises changed as the generations moved forward.

Grandfather Jory and Moriah lived a good long life together. They went on to have seven children. Throughout the years, as every child from that union was born, it was not known if it would be a fairy child and take after Moriah or a mortal such as Jory's side e of the family. And although it is true that one is not aware if their offspring has fairy traits until a child is at least seven years of age, there is always hope. Because to be born from a generation that sprouts wings can mean a lifetime of beauty contained within a mission to bring whimsy to the world, especially to anyone suffering a dark season. It is quite an honour to be the carrier of this duty, indeed, a gift to be cherished. And no one knew that better than Jory and Moriah's great, great granddaughter Daylen, who had birthed three beautiful fairy lasses and was now in waiting with another child.

Born on a breezy Autumn day, Rose was a tiny stunning creature with burnished red hair and bright green eyes. As she grew, she spent her days playing and running upon the cliffs that stretched out as far as your eyes could see. She and her sisters Kyrie, Emma and Mara would daily tend to the garden with their mother Daylen and toss out a crab pot or a fishing line or two. Every so often they would see a band of wild horse on the far side of the cliffs, running free. They were breathtaking.

Many days of splendour on these coastal cliffs, and always, there was abundance of life, love and provision for their little family.

In the Spring just before Rose turned seven her mother was thrilled to see tiny bits of wings appear. What a blessing to her mother! When wings begin to sprout, it is evidence that this child will do wonderful and selfless things for others, a blessing indeed!

As she grew, Rose's laugh could be heard echoing upon the cliffs and out towards the sea, even down into town on a stormy breezy day. Those were Rose's favourite days of all. She lived for a fierce wind that would rustle through the trees that lined the cliffs and play upon the long grasses of the land. A strong gust could float her up into the air, sometimes high enough to glimpse far of to the little town of Ballon, where her heart had found a boy. Not a fairy such as she, but a real boy, one without wings. When her mother would take her to town with her to get supplies, she would see him but was too shy to speak. She would hide, summoning up the courage to peek around a corner or two at his sweet face.

When the sun would go down father would return from his day's work. Before the season of rains, and only after supper when all the chores were done, father would build a lovely fire for them to gather by at the edge of the cliffs. The sound of the sea below crashing on the rocks was soothing and healing. The night would come to life with father on his banjo and mother on her mandolin. They would play and sing as Rose, Kyrie, Mara and Emma would join in with lovely harmonies that only fairies knew how to sing. Dancing beautiful dances, they were becoming young ladies, now in their teens. They danced with their feet barely touching the ground with joy and laughter, as their hearts as well as their wings grew stronger with each and every year.

As the evenings would grow to a close, family time gatherings were ended with their favourite song, the Fairy Song:

Hand made lace & pumpkin pies
Bringing hope to those that sigh
And sparkle dust for those that cry
Brightly lit with laughter and love
Heart of grace bestowed from above
Sweet sweet unending love
Is what a Celtic Fairy is made of

Off in the distance, down the hill, Rylee, the boy without wings would stand at the edge of town and could hear them laughing and singing. The sound of the girls' song was faint, he could just barely hear it on the wind as he stood in the distance. But is heart was touched as it would swell in his chest. He was in love with the young girl who hid behind her mother when they came to town. Standing at the edge of town he could see a tiny fire on the cliffs above, and he knew that the girl he loved was there among the merriment. Yes, indeed he had only seen her a few times, but she was the one.

Through the winter months Rose and her sisters Kyrie, Emma and Mara would gather in Rose's room nestled just inside the grand balcony. They spent these evenings telling stories and singing songs, braiding each others hair and speaking of good deeds planned for the villagers who were in need of aid, due to various ailments and unkindly circumstances they had unfortunately fallen into. They were positive and tender hearted as they sang songs about heaven, about angels, and wonderful deeds to be done. One could feel the atmosphere charged with beauty and light. Evenings such as these, were the perfect time to spread their wings, stretching them forth without onlookers possibly catching a glimpse. A time to gather and reflect on a mission of kindness and pla days of servantship towards their fellow neighbours.

Suddenly, Mara says in a hushed voice "Do you hear that? What is that?" Tap tap tap, tap tap tap.

The four of them crept to the window, cautiously peeking out through lacy curtains. There, sitting on the railing was a small white dove with something dangling from its neck. Rose picked up her ring of keys, slowly unlocked the door to the balcony and tip-toed out towards this lovely creature, speaking softly as she moved. She could see that it was carrying a shiny gold ribbon. Reaching out, she gently untied the precious ribbon as the bird patiently waited. The task was done, holding it in her hand it sparkled in the moonlight as the bird took flight. What may this be? Rose wondered. This indeed was a treasure. One that could only come from a far away land, for she had never seen this kind of opulence before.

There were no answers to this visitation, none. The following night the sisters gathered in Rose's room once more, just to see if perhaps this lovely bird would return. They were not to be disappointed. There it was, that sound, tap tap, tap tap tap, this time they all heard it. As rose opened the multicoloured stained glass door she saw two white doves, both with something tied to their necks. Oh what a delight as she untied these treasures from their necks! One carried a small charm in the shape of a heart, the other, a tiny scroll. Rose brought her treasures back into her room and read to her sisters from the tiny scroll:

Rose, my light, my love
Although you do not know me
I have loved you from afar
Although you have not known me
I have given you my life, my heart
Forever I will be yours

Stunned and mystified Rose could not imagine who this came from. "Who is it that loves me so?" Rose gushed to her sisters. "How can this be? Could it be the one I love? Could it be the boy without wings?"

From that night forth in that winter season, she waited in her room for a feathered message or trinket to be delivered. There would be many more nights that she would receive tiny notes of love, pieces of fine linen, silver trinkets and sweet treasures. But it would not be until the winter frost had gone and the solstice season was upon them, that the mystery of the doves and the one who loved her would be revealed.

Twas a balmy night with the illusive appeal of the solstice season as she stood on her balcony with all of her hidden desires and unspoken battles. This is the place where she gazed at a star filled sky and dreams spoke to her from her heart. Here she could be alone and weep if needed, or simply breath. Yes, it was a fine life living in this dwelling with a family she loved with all of her heart, but Rose never told them that her deepest desire was to adventure out to the depths of the sea on a ship carrying treasures and provisions to help others. Her destiny was to be a light to a world in need. She heard the stories of a kingdom across the waters that suffered war. She knew in her heart that they were desperately in need. Surely, she could explain this to her family. Wasn't it the duty of a fairy to bring love and hope to those in need? Oh, she wanted to do much more than that. Rose wanted to bring handmade items of cloth and quilts, pottery and dried berries, hand made musical instruments and juniper, burdock and nettle. All of what could heal spirit, soul and body. All of what could help to restore and make a kingdom whole again.

She stood in the moonlight dreaming. In her imagination she could see a sturdy ship being loaded and hear the goodbyes from her family as she set sail, off to another land.

Suddenly Rose heard rustling down below her balcony, in the thickets. It must have been the wind or her imagination she thought, as she watched the tall trees swaying in such a gentle sweet breeze. Or perhaps it was a dove, waiting for the perfect moment to light on her balcony. Dismissing the noise, she went back to her thoughts and knew in her heart that this was the night she must make a decision to tell her family of her dreams. This would be the night that clarity would visit, where vital decisions would be settled and she would put a plan in place, a plan to lay out her destiny before them, she was just sure of it.

Again Rose heard a rustling below. Looking down for her moonlit balcony, there, in the shadows, a figure hiding in the dark amongst the thicket. Stepping out into the moonlight, it was the boy without wings. He looked so handsome in the moonlit night! Her heart was pounding, it was her young man from town, her secret love! Rose leaned against the banister, feeling her heart swell with love. But what could he be doing here?

He moved a few step closer and said boldly "Pardon me my sweet one, I did not mean to frighten you. Please dear one, my name is Rylee, may I speak with you? I have seen you come to town with your mother, and from a distance I have heard your merriment in the evening when you and your family gather around the fire."

"Whyyyyyy, yes." Rose stammered. "If it pleases you to speak dear sir, please do so."

"Beautiful one, lovely Rose, I have seen you from afar, and I have seen you hiding before my eyes when you come to town with your mother. I inquired among the towns people of your name. I know in my heart, hat you are a sweet as a summer rain, and that your heart is as pure as a winter's snow. It is I that have sent doves to your balcony with messages of love." Rylee said gallantly, removing his hat, now bowing.

Rose could hardly breath, it was him! It was him! The love of her dreams had sent such precious things!

"I have come to ask you to accompany me on a journey. You see, my father's mercantile is chartering a ship to sail across the sea and bring provision to a land where people are suffering. Will you please consider joining me? If it is marriage that your require to do so, I shall want it with all of my heart!" Rylee said sincerely, bowing again below her. "Please my love, consider my words. In a fortnight I shall send a dove to your balcony, and please my love, please return to me a letter in reply to my words which I have spoken here this night. With this, I bid you farewell, until your words reach me." Rylee turned and vanished into the night.

It was late, and Rose was aflutter. Leaving th
frostiness of the night, she stepped back into he
chamber closing the balcony door tightly behind he
Rushing through her lace clad chamber, her wing
unfolded as she practically flew to her sisters Emma
Mara and Kyrie's chamber.

"Sister, whatsoever are you in such a twitter about?
Whispered Emma.

"Come to my chamber Emma, I must speak to yo
and Kyrie." Rose gushed.

Yes, getting out of a warm winter bed on col
December night would be nothing less than completel

miraculous. Emma and Kyrie wrapped themselves in blankets and Rose wrapped herself in a warm wool quilt that was handmade by her grandmother. Taking just a moment to tuck her other sister snugly in, for Mara was much too sleepy to care about such excitement.

Gathered in Rose's chamber, bundled next to the glowing embers, Kyrie was chosen to step out on the chilly balcony to find a good solid log of wood for the fire, so the sisters could stay warm. A mysterious excitement was about to unfold as the youngest sister began to untangle her many thoughts and feelings. She poured her heart about deep things, telling of the love she had for the boy without wings, who lived and worked in the city. The sisters sat quietly as Rose chatted enthusiastically about the events of Rilee's visit, and his pleas of love and promises of adventure.

Emma piped up almost shouting, "Oh you must, you must go with him Rose! You simply must!"

Then Kyrie spoke up, "Yes Rose, how can you not follow these deep desires of your heart? And this union is for the good of the people, which is your duty!"

Rose pondered their words as her sisters left her chambers. She could hear them as they went whispering gayly down the hall. Although she felt she may never get to sleep, it was not long before Rose awoke in the wee hours, even before the morning light summoned. Her first thought was to tell her mother and father, but then she took a moment to search her heart, "Is he truly where my heart shall light, is this the way my soul's desire shall go?" But she already knew the answer.

Before mother could arise to assist her daughters in readying breakfast, Rose was at her door, knocking. "Please do come in Rose." Her mother said sleepily.

"Mum, father, I have something to discuss with you, if I may." Speaking softly and bowing ever so slightly as she entered the room.

"Yes, Rose, please come sit on our bed and do tell us what is on your mind." Daylen yawned, offering as she patted the lush silk quilt covering their bed. Father on the other side, rustled under his covers.

Rose sat next to her mum, she had much to tell her. About the winter doves, about the mysterious notes they brought to her balcony, and about the visitation of the boy without wings and his desire to be in service to others across the great sea. Rilee was someone her mother not only knew, but one she was quite aware that her daughter had been sweet on for years now.

"Oh dear Rose! You must not go!" Mother gushed. "It was upon a great ship that your grandfather perished in the wild and wicked sea! You shall not go! What if the dark past comes to us again and we lose you sweet daughter? This I could not bear!"

Father now chiming in, "Rose, my beautiful little fairy, you are seventeen now, your next birth celebration comes hence in the Fall. You are not of age to be making decisions on the myriad of promises this young man Rilee has spoken. And what if you discovered, that across the sea there is a land full of giants? You shall not go my dear, you way is not certain, this I shall forbid!"

Disheartened Rose left her parents chambers. How is it that they do not understand the depth of her vision within the calling? How could they not see that she was, very much, in love?

Within the next few moons the season of planting crops was on the minds of the townspeople and Rose's family began to till the soil until it was readied. Tired and sore from working the land, Rose retired to her chambers, only to be woken by a dove, tapping at her widow. As she opened her doors she could see a note tied with string to the bird's neck. Retrieving it gently she unrolled the tiny note. On it was written:

The spontaneous pounding of Rose's heart was utterly blissful! How could it be that he loves me so? I must be with him, yes, forever! In the Earrach (Spring) which was shortly away, Rilee would be sailing with provision to those in need. I must go with him! He is my love, my destiny!

Rose spent the next few months secretly readying herself and her belongings. Not wanting to be against her parent's wishes, but knowing in her heart she must go. She gingerly crept about gathering all provisions she would need. The next time a dove flew to her balcony with the writings of love, she was ready with a note of her own.

t would be a long fortnight without doves returning a message from her love. It would not be until one beautiful Celtic evening while Rose was taking a walk in the garden, *i solas na gealaí* (in the moonlight), alone in contemplation. Through the trees lining the land, she saw a figure appear. It was Rilee, it was him! He saw her and quickened his gate until reaching her, grabbing her into his arms and kissing her passionately. Rose felt herself melt, yes it was truly love! Blissfully, they were finally together, their love had been sealed with a kiss.

Rilee, caressing Rose's face in his hands whispered, let us leave this night. I have taken possession of a vessel for voyage. It has been filled with provision and sealed with my father's blessings. We shall wed when we arrive across the great waters."

Rose could feel herself blushing, she shyly bowed her head, for this had been her first kiss, and now an official proposal of marriage? She shyly responded, yes my love, so do I wish it to be. Tho I do not have the assurance of my mother and father."

We must speak with them in the morrow, together. Yes, together we shall state our intentions." Rilee was speaking adamant declarations.

Early that morning when Rose's parents came downstairs, Rilee and Rose were waiting. They sat with them in their bountiful kitchen surrounded by all her sisters, and a pet or two. It was there that they laid out their well conceived plan about the voyage and to reassure Rose's father that Rilee had it on the strictest authority that giants truly did not exist in the land on the other shore of the Celtic Sea.

Rose's father was the first to speak."This is a solid plan, set on a solid foundation by a young man that has quickly gained my admiration. If this is the desire of my dearest young daughter, then today, before the sun sleeps, there shall be a wedding!"

Rose and Rilee were elated! The family leapt to their feet shouting in joy. A wedding it shall be!

They gathered newly blossoming flowers and ribbons for Rose's hair. Her mother's gown was gathered from the family cedar chest, freshened and fitted. It was father and Mara's task to go to town to fetch Father Kelly, and let the townspeople know of the impending nuptial that eve. It would be ten short hours before the glorious occasion. This would be a day of rejoicing, for when the sun arose, Rose and Rilee would leave.

That evening, the garden was lined and lit with

many candles as the brilliant orange sun began to set across the great Celtic Sea. Rose was illuminated by candle light as she walked down the linen clad isle towards Father Kelly. Rilee was glowing with anticipation. Rose's father bowed and offered him his beloved daughter as she softly reached out and took Rilee's arm. Rilee gazed at her intently glowing. This was to be his beautiful forever bride, the desires of their heart about to become one. And in the morrow they would begin to realize their dream of setting sail on their mission of light and love. But tonight the biggest surprise of all, Rilee would discover a secret his of his newly betrothed he had not yet discovered . . . ♡

The End

ABOUT THE AUTHOR

Warrior Danika is a Christian Celtic Warrior that stands for justice, peace and worldwide brotherly love.

Being left behind at birth by her Celtic gypsy clan, she was adopted and raised by a strong Irish family in the outskirts of Seattle. There she spent her early years playing in the woods where she gained a rich appreciation for the living breathing forest fantasy world that surrounded her. Deep within the trees was where she felt at home most, a sanctuary where she found peace in her destined solitary existence.

It was her great love for the tranquillity the forest that created and fanned a flame of passion in her heart. She spent her childhood among old growth trees, sheer cliffs, delightful animated creatures, and hidden bodies of water. The most perfect of all days was when the wind would blaze through the trees, creating a rushing symphony of wonder, a delight to her senses, making reality, perfect in every way.

She is a hard rock lead singer and a Digital Cyber Artist. It is out of many blessings and her life experiences that whimsical stories have come forth and are now being shared for all to enjoy!

Warrior Danika Media Info:

REVERBNATION
www.reverbnation.com/warriordanika

WEBSITE
warriordanika.com

INSTAGRAM
www.instagram.com/warriordanika

TWITTER
twitter.com/WarriorDanika7

EMAIL
warriordanika@gmail.com